# BAKING
# DAY
## ~ at ~
# GRANDMA'S

## Anika Denise

### illustrated by Christopher Denise

*Philomel Books*  An Imprint of Penguin Group (USA)

*I*t's baking day!
It's baking day!
It's baking day at Grandma's!

Bundle up—it's time to go
out across the drifts of snow.

Past the pond, so smooth and clear,

little cottage drawing near.

Knock-knock-knock on Grandma's door.
Hear her pad across the floor.
Plant a kiss on Grandma's nose,
cozy fire, warming toes.

It's baking day!
It's baking day!
It's baking day at Grandma's!

Pass out aprons, "One-two-three."
Grandma reads the recipe:
flour, sugar, butter, eggs.
Stand on chairs with tippy legs.

Wooden spoon and measuring cup,
mix the batter; stir it up.
Fold it gently in the pan,
lick the spoon because we can.

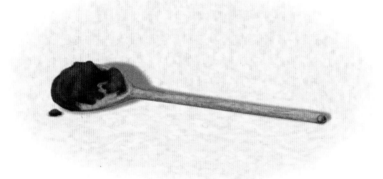

It's baking day!
It's baking day!
It's baking day at
Grandma's!

Hop down from the tippy chair,
smell the sweetness in the air.
One hot cocoa at each place.
Frosty window, smiley face.

Old-time music, soft and sweet.
Skippy notes and tapping feet.
Learning songs that Grandma sings—
when the kitchen timer rings!

It's baking day!
It's baking day!
It's baking day at
Grandma's!

Flip the pan, and out it pops!
Cut in squares and frost the tops.
Add some sprinkles, wrap each one,
tie a ribbon, nearly done.

Tasty treats in pretty bags,
each one marked with little tags.
Coats and boots and hats and gloves,
the hugs we know that Grandma loves.

It's baking day!
It's baking day!
It's baking day at Grandma's!

Walking home under the moon.

# Grandma Rosie's Chocolate Cake

| | | |
|---|---|---|
| 1 cup sugar | pinch of salt | 1 tsp. baking soda |
| ½ cup cocoa | 4 Tbsp. butter (half a stick) | 1 egg |
| 1 cup flour | 1 cup boiling hot water | 1 tsp. vanilla |

- Preheat the oven to 350 degrees.
- Mix the sugar, cocoa, flour and salt in a large bowl.
- Using a small spoon, make a hollow in the center of the mixture.
- Add the butter in slices to the hollow center.
- Stir the baking soda into the cup of boiling water. While it foams, pour it over the butter. Let the mixture sit until the butter melts and the batter cools.
- Add the egg and vanilla to the bowl and mix all the ingredients well.
- Pour the batter into a lightly greased 9x9 baking pan and bake at 350 degrees for 30-35 minutes.
- Test with a cake tester. The tester should come out dry.
- Allow the cake to cool after baking, then frost and enjoy!

Always ask an adult to help you.

*For my mom, Laurie, and for Grandma Rose.   —AD*

*For my mom.   —CD*

## PHILOMEL BOOKS

Published by the Penguin Group | Penguin Group (USA) LLC
375 Hudson Street, New York, NY 10014

USA | Canada | UK | Ireland | Australia | New Zealand | India | South Africa | China
penguin.com   A Penguin Random House Company

Text copyright © 2014 by Anika Denise.
Illustrations copyright © 2014 by Christopher Denise Illustrator Inc.
Library of Congress Cataloging-in-Publication Data
Denise, Anika.
Baking day at Grandma's / Anika Denise ; illustrated by Christopher Denise.   pages cm
Summary: "Children go to their grandmother's house to bake and enjoy spending time with their loving grandmother"—Provided by publisher.
[1. Stories in rhyme. 2. Grandmothers—Fiction. 3. Baking—Fiction.] I. Denise, Christopher, illustrator.
II. Title.  PZ8.3.D43165Bak 2014  [E]—dc23  2013031124  Manufactured in China by South China Printing Co. Ltd.
ISBN 978-0-399-24244-1  10 9 8 7 6 5 4 3 2 1

Design by Semadar Megged. | Text set in 27-point CooperOldStyURWTOTLig. | The art was created using Adobe Photoshop.

Back to visit Grandma soon.